D0894445

A Dance for Emilia

PETER S. BEAGLE

A DANCE FOR EMILIA

A ROC BOOK

ROC
Published by New American Library, a division of
Penguin Putnam Inc., 375 Hudson Street, New York, New York 10014, U.S.A.
Penguin Books Ltd, 27 Wrights Lane, London W8 5TZ, England
Penguin Books Australia Ltd, Ringwood, Victoria, Australia
Penguin Books Canada Ltd, 10 Alcorn Avenue, Toronto, Ontario, Canada M4V 3B2
Penguin Books (N.Z.) Ltd, 182–190 Wairau Road, Auckland 10, New Zealand

Penguin Books Ltd, Registered Offices: Harmondsworth, Middlesex, England

First published by Roc, an imprint of New American Library,
a division of Penguin Putnam Inc.

First Printing, October 2000
10 9 8 7 6 5 4 3 2 1

LIBRARY OF CONGRESS CATALOGING-IN-PUBLICATION DATA:
Beagle, Peter S.
A dance for Emilia / Peter S. Beagle.
p. cm.
ISBN 0-451-45800-1 (alk. paper)
1. Friendship—Fiction. 2. Death—Fiction. 3. Cats—Fiction. I. Title.
PS3552.E13 D36 2000
813'.54—dc21 00-031096

Printed in the United States of America
Set in Sabon
Designed by Julian Hamer

For Nancy, Peter and Jessa,
and for Joe

A Dance for Emilia

The cat. The cat is doing what?

Believe me, it's no good to tell you. You have to see.

Emilia, she's old. Old cats get really weird sometimes.

Not like this. You have to see, that's all.

You're serious. You're going to put Millamant in a box, a case, and bring her all the way to California, just for me to . . . When are you coming?

I thought Tuesday. I'm due ten days' sick leave. . . .

No. This isn't how you do it. This isn't how you talk about Sam and Emilia and yourself. And Millamant. You've got hold of the wrong end, same as usual. Start from the beginning. For your own sake, tell it, just write it down the way it was, as far as you'll ever know. Start with the answering machine. That much you're sure about, anyway. . . .

The machine was twinkling at me when I came home from the Pacific Rep's last-but-one performance of *The Iceman Cometh*. I ignored it. You can live with things like computers, answering gadgets, fax machines, even e-mail, but they have to know their place. I hung up my coat, checked the mail, made myself a drink, took it and the newspaper over to the one comfortable chair I've got, sank down in it, drank my usual toast to our lead—who is undoubtedly off playing Hickey in Alaska today, feeding wrong cues to a cast of polar bears—and finally hit the PLAY button.

"Jacob, it's Marianne. In New York." I only hear from Marianne Hooper at Christmas these days, but we've known each other a long time, in the odd, offhand way of theater people, and there's no mistaking that husky, incredibly world-weary sound—she's been making a fortune doing voice-overs for the last twenty years. There was a pause. Marianne could always get more mileage out of a well-timed pause than Jack Benny. I raised my glass to the answering machine.

"Jacob, I'm so sorry, I hate to be the one to tell you. Sam was found dead in his apartment last night. I'm so sorry."

It didn't mean anything. It bounced off me—*it didn't mean anything*. Marianne went on. "People at the magazine got worried when he didn't come in to work, didn't answer the phone for two days. They finally broke into the apartment." The famous anonymous voice was trembling now. "Jacob, I'm so terribly . . . Jacob, I can't do this anymore, on a machine. Please call me." She left her number and hung up.

I sat there. I put my drink down, but otherwise I didn't move. I sat very still where I was, and I thought, *There's been a mistake. It's his turn to call me on Saturday, I called last week. Marianne's made a mistake.* I thought, *Oh, Christ, the cat, Millamant—who's feeding Millamant?* Those two, back and forth, over and over.

I don't know how late it was when I finally got up and phoned Marianne, but I know I woke her. She said, "I called you last. I called his parents before I could make myself call you."

"He was just here," I said. "In July, for God's sake. He was fine." I had to heave the words up one at a time, like prying stones out of a wall. "We went for walks."

"It was his heart." Marianne's voice was so toneless and uninflected that she sounded like someone else. "He was in the bathroom—he must have just come home from Lincoln Center—"

"The Schönberg. He was going to review that concert *Moses und Aron*—"

"He was still wearing his gangster suit, the one he always wore to openings—"

I was with him when he bought that stupid, enviable suit. I said, "The Italian silk thing. I remember."

Marianne said, "As far as they—the police—as far as anyone can figure, he came home, fed the cat, kicked off his shoes, went into the bathroom and—And died." She was crying now, in a hiccupy, totally unprofessional way. "Jacob, they think it was instant. I mean, they don't think he suffered at all."

I heard myself say, "I never knew he had a heart condition. Secretive little fink, he never told me."

Marianne managed a kind of laugh. "I don't think he ever told anyone. Even his mother and father didn't know."

"The cigarettes," I said. "The goddamn cigarettes. He was here last summer, trying to cut down—he said his doctor had scared the hell out of him. I just thought, *lung cancer, he's afraid of getting cancer.* I never thought about his heart, I'm such an idiot. Oh, God, I have to call them, Mike and Sarah."

"Not tonight, don't call them tonight." She'd been getting the voice back under control, but now it went again. "They're in shock; I did it to them, don't you. Wait till morning. Call them in the morning."

My mouth and throat were so dry they hurt, but I couldn't pick up my drink again. I said, "What's being done? You have to notify people, the police. I don't even know if he had a will. Where's the—Where is he now?"

"The police have the body, and the apartment's closed. Sealed—it's what they do when somebody dies without a witness. I don't know what happens next. Jacob, can you please come?"

"Thursday," I said. "Day after tomorrow. I'll catch the redeye right after the last performance."

"Come to my place. I've moved, there's a guest room." She managed to give me an East Eighties address before the tears came again. "I'm sorry, I'm sorry, I've been fine all day. I guess it's just caught up with me now."

"I'm not quite sure why," I said. I heard Marianne draw in her breath, and I went on, "Marianne, *I'm* sorry, I know how cold that sounds, but you and Sam haven't been an item for—what?—twelve years? Fifteen? I mean, this is me, Marianne. You can't be the grieving widow, it's just not your role."

I've always said things to Marianne that I'd never say to anyone else—it's the only way to get her full attention. Besides, it made her indignant, which beat the hell out of maudlin. She said, "We always stayed friends, you know that. We'd go out for dinner, he took me to plays—he must have told you. We were *always* friends, Jacob."

Sam cried over her. It was the only time that I ever saw Sam cry. "Thursday morning, then. It'll be good to see you." Words, thanks, sniffles. We hung up.

I couldn't stay sitting. I got up and walked around the room. "Oh, you little bastard," I said aloud. "Kagan, you miserable, miserable *twit*, who said you could just leave? We had *plans*, we were going to be old together, you forgot about that?" I was shouting, bumping into things. "We were going to be these terrible, totally irresponsible old men, so elegant and mannerly nobody would ever believe we just peed in the potted palm. We were going to learn karate, enter the Poker World Series, moon our fiftieth high school reunion, sit in the sun at spring-training baseball camps—we had stuff to *do*! What the hell were you *thinking* of, walking out in the middle of the movie? You think I'm about to do all that crap alone?"

I don't know how long I kept it up, but I know I was still yelling while I packed. I didn't have another show lined up after *Iceman* until the Rep's *Christmas*

Carol went into rehearsal in two months, with Bob Cratchit paying my rent one more time. No pets to feed, no babies crying, no excuses to make to anyone . . . there's something to be said for being fifty-six, twice divorced and increasingly set in my ways. I'm a good actor, with a fairly wide range for someone who looks quite a bit like Mister Ed, but I've got no more ambition than I have star quality. Which may be a large part of the reason why Sam Kagan and I were so close for so long.

We met in high school, in a drama class. I already knew that I was going to be an actor—though of course it was Olivier back then, not Mister Ed. The teacher was choosing students at random to read various scenes, and we, sitting at neighboring desks, got picked for a dialogue from *Major Barbara*. I was Adolphus Cusins, Barbara's Salvation Army fiancé; Sam played Undershaft, the arms manufacturer. He wasn't familiar with the play, but I was, and with Rex Harrison, who'd played Cusins in the movie, and whose every vocal mannerism I had down cold. Yet when we faced off over Barbara's ultimate allegiance and Sam proclaimed, in an outrageously fragrant British accent, Undershaft's gospel of "money and gunpowder—freedom and power—command of life and command of death," there wasn't an eye in that classroom resting anywhere but on him. I may have known the play better than he, but he knew that it was a *play*. It was the first real acting lesson I ever had.

I told him so in the hall after class. He looked honestly surprised. "Oh, good *night*, Undershaft's easy, he's all one thing—in that scene, anyway." The astonishing accent was even riper than before. "Now Cusins is bloody tricky, Cusins is much harder to play." He grinned at me—God, were the cigarettes already starting to stain his teeth then?—and added, "You do a great early Harrison, though. Did you ever see *St. Martin's Lane*? They're running it at the Thalia all next week."

He was the first person I had ever met in my life who talked like me. What I mean by that is that both of us much preferred theatrical dialogue to ordinary Brooklyn conversation, theatrical structure and action to life as it had been laid out for us. It makes for an awkward childhood—I'm sure that's one reason I got into acting so young—and people like us learn about protective coloration earlier than most. And we tend to recognize each other.

Sam. He was short—notably shorter than I, and I'm not tall—with dark eyes and dark, wavy hair, the transparent skin and soft mouth of a child, and a perpetual look of being just about to laugh. Yet even that early on, he kept his deep places apart: when he did laugh or smile, it was always quick and mischievous and gone. The eyes were warm, but that child's mouth held fast—to what, I don't think I ever knew.

He was a much better student than I—if it hadn't been for his help in half my subjects, I'd still be in high school. Like me, he was completely uninterested in anything beyond literature and drama; quite unlike me, he accepted the existence of geometry, chemistry and push-ups, where I never believed in their reality for a minute. "Think of it as a role," he used to tell me. "Right now you're playing a student, you're learning the periodic table like dialogue. Some day, good *night*, you might have to play a math teacher, a coach, a mad scientist. Everything has to come in useful to an actor, sooner or later."

He called me Jake, as only one other person ever has. He was a gracious loser at card and board games, but a terrible winner, who could gloat for two days over a gin rummy triumph. He was the only soul I ever told about my stillborn older brother, whose name was Elias. I knew where he was buried—though I had not been told—and I took Sam there once. He was outraged when he learned that we never spoke of Elias at home, and made me promise that I'd celebrate Elias's birthday every year. Because of Sam, I've been giving my brother a private birthday party for more than forty years. I've only missed twice.

Sam had surprisingly large hands, but his feet were so tiny that I used to tease him, referring to them as "ankles with toes." It was a sure way to rile him, as nothing else would do. Those small feet mattered terribly to Sam.

He was a dance student, most often going directly

from last-period math to classes downtown. Wanting to dance wasn't something boys admitted to easily then—certainly not in our Brooklyn high school, where being interested in *anything* beside football, fighting and very large breasts could get you called a faggot. I was the one person who knew about those classes; and we were seniors, with a lot of operas, Dodgers games and old Universal horror movies behind us, before I actually saw him dance.

There was a program at the shabby East Village studio where he was taking classes three times a week by then. Two pianos, folding chairs, and a sequence of presentations by students doing solo bits or *pas de deux* from the classic ballets. Sam's parents were there, sitting quietly in the very last row. I knew them, of course, as well as any kid who comes over to visit a friend for an afternoon ever knows the grown-ups floating around in the background. Mike was a lawyer, fragile-looking Sarah an elementary-school teacher; beyond that, all I could have said about them—or can say now—was that they so plainly thought their only child was the entire purpose of evolution that it touched even my hard adolescent heart. I can still see them on those splintery, rickety chairs: holding hands, except when they tolerantly applauded the fragments of *Swan Lake* and *Giselle*, waiting patiently for Sam to come onstage.

He was next to last on the program—the traditional starring slot in vaudeville—performing his own choreography to the music of Borodin's *In the Steppes Of Central Asia*. And what his dance was like I cannot tell you now, and I couldn't have told you then, dumbly enthralled as I was by the sight of my lunchroom friend hurling himself about the stage with an explosive ferocity that I'd never seen or imagined in him. Some dancers cut their shapes in the air; some burn them; but Sam tore and clawed his, and seemed literally to leave the air bleeding behind him. I can't even say whether he was *good* or not, as the word is used—though he was unquestionably the best in that school, and more people than his parents were on their feet when he finished. What I did somehow understand, bright and blind as I was, was that he was dancing for his life.

When I went backstage, he was sitting alone on a bench in his sweat-blackened leotard, head bowed into his hands. He didn't look up until I said, "Boy, that was something else. *You* are something else." The phrase was fairly new then, in our circles at least.

He looked old when he raised his head. I don't mean older; I mean old. The glass-clear skin was gray, pebbled with beard stubble—I hadn't thought he shaved—and the dark eyes appeared too heavy for his face to bear. He said slowly, "Sometimes I'm good, Jake. Sometimes I really think I might make it."

I said something I hadn't at all thought to say. "You have to make it. I don't think there's a damn thing else you're fit for."

Sam laughed. Really laughed, so that some color came back into his face and his eyes became his age again. "Good *night*, let's just hope I never have to find out." He got dressed and we went out front to meet Mike and Sarah.

He didn't have to find out for some time. We

graduated, and I went off to Carnegie Tech in Pittsburgh on a genuine theater scholarship, while Sam stayed home, attending CCNY to please his parents, and literally spending all the rest of his time at Garrett-Klieman, a dance school whose top prospects seemed to be funneled directly into the New York City Ballet. I'd see him on holidays and over the summer, and we'd do everything we'd always done together: going to plays and baseball games, hitting the secondhand bookstores on Fourth Avenue, drinking beer and debating whether the internal rhymes in the songs we were always trying to write were as clever and crackling as Noël Coward's. On Friday nights, we usually played poker with a mixed bag of other would-be actors and dancers. As far as either of us was willing to acknowledge, nothing at all had changed.

But while I talked about plays I'd been in, about Artaud, Brecht, the Living Theatre, the Method, improv workshops and sense memories, Sam avoided almost all mention of his own career. If he danced in any of the Garrett-Klieman showcases, he never told me—it was all I could do to persuade him to let me sit in on a couple of his choreography classes. As before, I couldn't look away from him for a moment; but I was already beginning to learn that some dancers, actors, musicians simply have that. It doesn't have a thing to do with talent or craft—it just *is*, like blue eyes or being able to touch your nose with your tongue. I don't have it.

We were eating lunch at the Automat on Forty-second and Sixth the day he told me abruptly, "They haven't recommended me. Not to City Ballet, not to anybody. It's over."

I gaped at him over my crusty brown cup of baked beans. I said, "What *over*? This is crazy. You're the best dancer I ever knew."

"You don't know any dancers," Sam said. Which was perfectly true—I still don't know many; I'm not in a lot of musicals—but irritating under the circumstances. Sam went on, "They didn't tell me it was over. I knew. I'm not good enough."

I was properly outraged, not only at Garrett-Klieman, but also at him, for acceding so docilely to their decision. I said, "Well, the hell with them. What the hell do *they* know?"

Sam shook his head. "Jake, I'm not good enough. It's that simple."

"Nothing's that simple. You've been dancing all your life, you've been the best everywhere you've gone—"

"I was *never* the best!" The Noël Coward accent had dropped away for the first time in my memory, and Sam's voice was all aching Brooklyn. "You remember that story you told me about Queen Elizabeth—the real one—that thing she said when she was old. 'No, I was never beautiful, but I had the name for it.' It was like that with me. I can be dazzling—I worked on it, I about killed myself learning to be dazzling—but there isn't a move in me that I didn't copy from d'Amboise or Bruhn or Eddie Villella or someone. And these people aren't fools, Jake. They know the difference between dazzling and dancing. So do I."

I didn't know how to answer him; not because of what he had said, but because of the utter nakedness of his voice. He stared at me in silence for a long time, and then suddenly he looked away, the break so sharp that it felt physical, painful. He said, "Anyway, I'm too short."

I laughed. I remember *that*. "What are you talking about? Even I know ballet dancers can't be tall—Villella's practically a midget, for God's sake—"

"No, he's not. And he's strong as a horse; he can lift his partners all day and not break a sweat. I can't do that." All these years, and I can still see the absolute, unarguable shame in his face. "My upper body's never going to be strong enough to do what it has to do. And I look wrong onstage, Jake. My legs are stubby, they spoil the line. It *is* that bloody simple, and I'm very glad someone finally laid it out for me. Now all I have to do is figure out what exactly to do with the rest of my life."

He stood up and walked out of the Automat, and by the time I got outside, he was gone. We didn't see each other for the rest of the summer, although we talked on the phone a couple of times. By then, thanks to sending out ninety-four sets of resumés, I actually had a job waiting for me after graduation, building sets and doing walk-ons for a rep company in Seattle. Over the next five years I worked my way down to the Bay Area, by way of theaters in Eugene and Portland and stock jobs all over Northern California. I've been here in Avicenna ever since.

But we did stay in contact, Sam and I. I broke the ice, sending light postcards from the summer tours, and then a real letter from my first real address—South Parnell Street, that was. Two rooms and a ficus plant.

He didn't answer for some while, long enough that I began to believe he never would. But when it did come, the letter began with typical abruptness, asking whether I remembered *The Body Snatcher*, an old Val Lewton movie we'd loved and seen half a dozen times.

> Remember that splendid, chilling moment when Karloff says through his teeth, "And I have done some things that I did not want to do . . ."? Me these last several years. I'll tell you the worst

> straight off, and leave the rest to your imagination. No, not the year spent teaching folk-dancing in Junior High School 80—much worse than that. I am become an Arts Cricket! Pray for me. . . .

We'd been using Gully Jimson's term for a critic ever since reading *The Horse's Mouth* in high school. Sam's letter went on to say that he was writing regularly for a brand-new Manhattan arts magazine, now and then for a couple of upstate papers, and lately even filing occasional dispatches to Japan:

> I mostly review music, sometimes theater, sometimes movies, if the first-stringer's off at Sundance or Cannes. No, Jake, I don't ever cover dance. I don't dare write about dance, because I couldn't possibly be fair to people who are up there doing what I want to do more than I want anything in the world. Music, yes. I can manage music. . . .

We wrote, and sometimes called, for another three years before we met again. I hope my letters weren't as full of myself as I'm sure they were: entirely concerned with what plays I'd auditioned for, what roles I should have gotten, what actors I scorned or admired; what celebrated director had seemed very impressed but never called back. Sam, on the other hand, recounted the astonishing success of *Ceilidh*, the new magazine, described every editor and photographer he worked with; detailed, with solemn hilarity, the kind of performance he was most often sent to cover. "Most of them are so far *avant* that they lap the field and become the *derrière-garde*. Try to imagine the Three Stooges on downers."

But of his own feelings and dreams, of his world beyond work, of how he lived without dancing—nothing, not ever. And there we left it until I came to New York for a smallish part in a goodish play that survived barely a month. It was to be my Broadway break, that one—to be in it I turned down a TV movie, which later spun off into a syndicated series that's probably still running somewhere. I have an infallible gift for picking the losing side.

I never regretted the gamble, though, for I stayed

with Sam during our brief run. He had found a studio apartment in the West Seventies, half a block off Columbus: one huge, high room, a vestigial kitchen nook, a bathroom, a deep and sinister coat closet that Sam called "The Dark Continent," a solid wall of books, the two biggest stereo speakers I'd ever seen, and a mattress in a far corner. I slept on the floor by the stereo that month, in a tangle of quilts from his Brooklyn bedroom. It was the first time we'd ever spent together as adults, with jobs to go to instead of classes. We kept completely different hours, what with me being at the theater six nights and two afternoons a week, while Sam put in five full days at the magazine, and was likely to be off covering a performance in the evenings. Yet we bumbled along so comfortably that I can't recall a cross word between us—only an evening when something changed.

At the time I was skidding into my first marriage, a head-on collision, born of mutual misunderstandings, with the woman who was lighting the play. On the windy, rainy evening that the closing notice was posted, she and I had a fight about nothing, and I sulked my way back to Sam's place to find him practicing a Bach sarabande on his classical guitar. He wasn't very good, and he wouldn't ever be good, no matter how dutifully he worked at it, and to my shame I said so that night. "Give it up, Sam. You haven't made a dent in that poor Bach in all the time I've been here. Guitar's just not your instrument—it's like me and directing. I can't even get three people lined up properly for a photograph. It's not the end of the world."

It helped a bit on the flight to New York, staring at the fold-down tray in front of me for five hours, to remember that Sam didn't pay the least bit of attention to me. When the sarabande had lurched to a close, he said, "Jake, I don't have any illusions about the way I play. But I don't think anyone should write about music who doesn't have at least some idea of what it takes to make your fingers pull one clear note out of an instrument. Out of yourself."

"The guitar you keep hacking at. The thing you could *do,* you quit. Right." I can still hear the pure damn meanness in my voice.

Sam put the guitar away and began rummaging in the refrigerator for a couple of beers. His back was to me when he said, "Yes, well, I did have some illusions about my dancing." He hadn't used the word all during my visit. "But that's what they were, Jake, illusions, and I'm glad I understood that when I did. I haven't lost any sleep over them in . . . what? Years."

"You were good," I said. "You were terrific." Sam didn't turn or answer. Completely out of character, out of control, I kept pushing. "Ever wish you hadn't quit?"

"I still dance." For the first time since that long-ago lunch in the Automat, the voice was raw Brooklyn again, but much lower, a harsh mumble. "I take classes, I keep in shape." He did turn to face me then, and now there was anger in his eyes. "And no, Jake, I don't wish a damn thing. I'm just grateful that I had the sense to know what to stop wishing for. I didn't quit, I let go. There's a difference."

"Is there?" What possessed me? what made me bait him, invade him so? The failure of the play, premonitions about my Lady of the Follow Spots? I have no more idea now than I did then. I said, "I've envied you half my life, you know that? You were born to be a dancer—*born*—and I've had to work my butt off just to be the journeyman I am." The words chewed their way out of me. "Sam, see, by now I know I'm never going to be anything more than pretty good. Professional, I'll settle for that. But you . . . you walked away from it, from your gift. I was so furious at you for doing that. I guess I still am. I really still am."

"That's your business," Sam said. His voice had gotten very quiet. "My loss is my loss, you don't get to deal yourself in. Sorry." He said it carefully, word by word, each one a branding iron. "I have enough trouble with my own dreams without living yours."

"What dreams?" I asked. He should have hit me then—not for the two words, but for the way I said them. I can still hear myself today, now, as I write this, and I am still ashamed.

But Sam smiled at me. Whatever else I manage to forget about my behavior that night, I'll always remember that he smiled. He said, "Anyway, you're a bloody good actor. You're much better than a journeyman." And he handed me a bottle of beer, and suddenly we were talking about my career, about me again. We weren't to have another moment that intense, that intimate, for a very long time.

Over the years I came east more often than he came west, unless he had a Seattle Opera *Ring* to cover, or a Los Angeles symphony conductor to interview. He published three books: one on a year spent with the musicians of the Lincoln Center orchestra, one on Lou Harrison, and one—my favorite—about Verdi's last four operas. They got fine reviews and neither sold nor stayed in print. But the studio apartment was rent-controlled, and *Ceilidh* flourished, to its own considerable surprise. Occasionally they were even able to send Sam abroad, to cover music festivals in England or Italy. He visited his parents—long retired in Fort Lauderdale—four times a year, had another floor-to-ceiling bookcase installed, and got a cat.

About the cat. It was an Abyssinian female, almost

maroon in color, and even as a kitten she had the slouchy preen of a high-fashion model. Sam named her Millamant, after Congreve's wicked heroine. Because both of the women I married had been cat-lovers, Sam appointed me his feline expert, and called me almost every day during the first weeks of Millamant's residency. "She just sits in her litter box and stares—is that normal?" "She keeps catching moths in The Dark Continent—should I make her stop?" "Jake, I took her for her shots, and now she's mad at me. How long do cats stay mad?" "Is it all right for her to eat pizza?" Millamant grew up to look like a miniature mountain lion, the reigning *grande horizontale* of the studio, and whenever I slept on the floor, she honored me with her favors. Usually at three in the morning.

As for myself, I peaked early. Right or wrong about Sam's talent, I was bang on the money about my own. I've never worked in New York again, unless you count summer stock in Utica, and there have been stretches when a voice-over, a TV cameo, or residuals from a soap-opera guest shot were all that kept a roof over my head. It's mostly theater, especially the Pacific Rep, that pays the bills; but the only long-running stage gig I have ever had was as a villain in a camp 1890s melodrama, which inexplicably ran for five years at a tiny San Francisco theater. It coincided almost exactly with my second marriage; they closed in the same week. That one's a director, and she's good. I think she's off doing *Sweet Bird of Youth* in China right now.

All the same, for good or ill, I'm still doing what I'm fit for and living as I always wanted to live—just not quite as well as I'd imagined—and Sam wasn't. That was a wider gap by far than the continent that separated us, but we never again talked about it. Everything else, yes, on weekends, when the rates were down—everything else from politics, literature and the general nature of the universe to shortstops and whether Oscar Aléman could really have been as good a guitarist as Django. We went along like that until Marianne.

No, we went along like that until *after* Marianne. After she'd moved in with him, and after she'd left him two months and five days later for a playwright who'd written a one-woman show about Duse for her. I borrowed plane fare to New York because of the way he sounded on the phone. He was fine all the way through the nice dinner at the deli, and fine through the usual amble along Columbus, twenty blocks or so down, twenty blocks back. It wasn't until we were in the apartment, until I'd found a hairbrush of Marianne's and casually asked him where I should put it, that he came apart. I held him awkwardly while he cried, and Millamant came down from the bookshelf where she generally lived to sniff at his tears and butt her hard round head against his chin. It was a very long night, and I don't know whether I did or said anything right or anything wrong for him. I was just with him, that's all.

He came to Avicenna more often after that, always spending at least a weekend, sleeping on a futon, content with my books and record albums if I was in rehearsal; ready for a walk on balmy evenings—he never quite lost the unmistakable near-waddle of the ballet dancer—equally easy with silences long grown as comfortable as the lazily circular arguments that might go on until one of us dozed off. I recall asking one midnight, during his last visit, "Do you remember what your dad used to say, every time he heard us discussing something or other?"

Sam laughed in the darkness. " 'Those two, they're a couple of *alte kockers* already! Old men sitting in the park, squabbling about Tennessee Williams and Mickey Mantle.' Fifteen, sixteen, and he had us pegged."

I remember everything about that visit, when he holed up in my house for a full week, trying so determinedly to quit smoking. The walks got longer, to keep his mind off cigarettes; he managed quite well during the daytime, but the nights were hard, as I could tell from the smell in the bathroom most mornings. Even so, he cut down steadily until, a couple of days before he left, he got by on two half-smoked cigarettes, and we went out to my favorite Caribbean restaurant to celebrate. He had the jerk chicken and I had the *rópa vieja*.

There's an unmarked alley not far from my house

that leads to a freeway overpass, and from there into a children's park as dainty and miniature as a scene in one of those gilded Victorian eggs. We walked there after dinner, talking obliquely of Marianne, for the first time in a long while, and of my ex-wives. It was when we stopped to drink at a child-size fountain that Sam said, "You know, when you think about it, you and I have been involved with a remarkable number of highly improbable women. I mean, for just two people."

"We could start a museum," I suggested. "The Museum of Truly Weird Relationships." That set us off: we walked round and round for hours, opening up the one aspect of our lives kept almost entirely private for all the years of our friendship. The public defender, the bookstore owner, the poet, the set designer, the truck mechanic—it doesn't matter which of us was embrangled with whom; only that the romances almost invariably ended as comedies of errors, leaving us to lick our wounds and shrug, and present our debacles to each other like wry trophies. We laughed and snorted, and said, "*What?*" and

"Oh, you're *kidding*" and "You never said a word about *that*—that's a whole wing of the museum just by itself," until the children and their parents were all gone home, and we were the only two voices in the little park. It was just then that Sam told me about Emilia.

"She's too young," he said. "She is twenty-six-and-a-half years younger than I am, and she's from Metuchen, New Jersey, and she's not Jewish, and if you say either *bimbo* or *bunnyrabbit*, Jake, I will punch you right in the eye. I shouldn't have mentioned her, anyway. I don't think this one belongs in the Museum at all."

"Hoo-*ha,*" I said. He looked at me, and I said, "Sorry, sorry, hoo-ha withdrawn—it's just I've never heard you sound like that. So. Would you maybe marry this one?"

"You're the chap who marries people. If I were the sort who gets married, I'd *be* married by now." He fell silent, and we walked on until we came to the swings and the sliding pond and the monkey bars. We sat down on the swings, pushing ourselves idly in small circles, letting our shoes scrape the ground. Sam said, "Emilia covers New York for a paper in Bergen County—that's how I met her, about a year ago. She takes the bus in on weekends."

"A journalist, yet. Not a cricket?"

"Good *night*, no, a real writer. If there were any real newspapers left, she'd have a real career ahead of her. I keep telling her to get into TV, but she hates it—she won't even watch the *News Hour*." He pushed off harder, gripping the chains of the swing and leaning back. "The whole thing's crazy, Jake, but it's not weird. It's just crazy." He looked over his shoulder at me and grinned suddenly. "But Millamant likes her."

"I'm jealous," I said, and I actually was, a little. Millamant doesn't like a lot of people. "She stays the weekend? And it works out?"

He was a heavy sleeper, and you had to be really careful about waking him, because he always came up fighting. I never knew why that was. Sam laughed then. "On top of everything, she's an insomniac. Only person I ever gave full permission to wake me up at any time. It works out."

"Hoo-*ha*. So she'll be moving in?"

Sam didn't answer for a long time. We swung together in the darkness, with no sound but the slow creak of the chains. Finally he said, "I don't think so. I think maybe I lost my nerve with Marianne." I started to say something, and then I didn't. Chains, owls, a few fireflies, the distant mumbling of the freeway. Sam said, "I couldn't go through that again. And it will happen again, Jake. Not for the same reasons, but it will."

"You don't know that," I said. "It works out sometimes, living with somebody. Not for me—I mean, both my marriages were absolute train wrecks—but there were good times even so, and they really might have worked. If I'd been different, or Elly had, or Suzette had. Anyway, it was worth it, pretty much. I wouldn't have missed it, I don't think."

"That," Sam said, pausing as precisely as our old hero Noël Coward would have done, "is the most inspirational tribute to the married state I've ever heard. You ought to crochet it into a sampler." He dropped lightly off the swing, and we went on walking, angling back the way we had come. Neither of us spoke again until we were on the overpass, looking down at the lights plunging toward the East Bay hills. Sam said, "She's not moving in. Millamant doesn't like her *that* much. But I want you to meet her, next time you come to New York. This one I want you to meet." I said I'd love to, and we walked on home.

At the airport, two nights later, we hugged each other, and I said, "Catch you next time, Jake." I don't remember when we started doing that at goodbyes, trading names.

"Next time, Sam. I'll call when I get home." He picked up his garment bag and started for the gate; then turned to flash me that fleeting grin out of childhood once more. "Keep a pedestal vacant in the Museum. You never know." And he was gone.

Marianne had Millamant, as it turned out when I made my way from JFK to her East Side town house. The Abyssinian met me at the door and immediately sprang to my shoulder, as she had always done whenever I arrived. Arthritis had set its teeth in her right hind leg since we last met, and it took her three tries, equally painful for us both. I tried to remove her, but Millamant wasn't having any. She dug her claws in even deeper, making a curious shrill sound I'd never heard from her before, and constantly pushing her head against my face. Her eyes were wide and mad.

"He's not with me," I said. "I'm sorry, cat. I don't know where he's gone."

Marianne—still all flying red hair and opening night, down to her gilded toenails—informed me that Sam hadn't left a will, which surprised me. He was always far neater than I, not merely about the apartment or his dress, but about his life in general. Letters were answered as they came in; his filing cabinet held actual alphabetized files; he always knew where his book and magazine contracts were; and he had a regular doctor and a real lawyer as well, who doubled as his literary agent. But there was no will in the filing cabinet, no will to be found anywhere.

"We'd been talking about it," the lawyer said defensively. "He was going to come in. Anyway, I've spoken to the parents, and they want you to act as executor."

I called Mike and Sarah from the lawyer's office. They were frail insect voices, clouded by age and distance and despair, static from deep space. Yes, they did wish me to be Sam's executor—yes, they would be grateful if I could clean out the apartment, sort his business affairs, and get the police to release his body, as soon as the coroner's report came in. Sarah asked after my mother and father.

The report said things like *myocardial infarction* and *ventricular fibrillation; death almost certainly instant.* We buried Sam in an Astroturf cemetery in Queens, within earshot of the Van Wyck Expressway. Mike and Sarah had managed to handle the funeral arrangements from Fort Lauderdale, which proved they remembered me well enough to know that I'd likely have wound up stashing their son in a Dumpster or a recycling bin. A limousine from the mortuary brought them to the funeral: they stepped out blinking against the sharp autumn sunlight, looking pale and small, for all the years in Florida. I went over to embrace them, and we had a moment to murmur incoherently together before two men in dark suits took them away to the grave site. I followed with Marianne, because there was no one else I knew.

It didn't surprise me. I'd learned long since that Sam preferred to keep the several worlds in which he moved—music, theater, journalism, ballet classes—utterly separate from each other. I'd known the names of some of his friends and colleagues for years, without ever meeting one. By the same token, I knew myself to be the entire mysterious, vaguely glamorous West Coast world into which he vanished once in a great while. Until now, it had all suited and amused me.

An old Friday-night poker acquaintance drifted up on my left as I stood at the coffin behind Mike and Sarah and the dark suits. We shook hands, and he whispered, "Yes, I know, I got fat," while I was still trying to remember his name. I never did.

The rabbi looked like a basketball player, and he hadn't known Sam. It was a generic eulogy, no worse for the most part than many I've sat through, until he fixed his shiny blue gaze on Mike and Sarah and started in about the tragedy of living to bury an only son. I turned away, eyeing the exits. *Damn, Sam, if you hadn't stuck us with these damn ringside seats, we could slide out of here right now, and be on the second beer before anyone noticed.* But he had to stay, so I did too.

That was when I saw the small dark woman standing alone. Not that she was physically isolated—you couldn't be in that crowd, and still see grave and rabbi—but her solitude, her apartness, was as plain as if she had been a homeless lunatic, trundling a Safeway cart, all by herself with God. She was looking at the rabbi, but not seeing or hearing him. I patted Marianne's arm and eased away. *It's okay, Sam. I see her.*

Close to, she was thin, and looked paler because of her dark hair and eyes. She looked older, too— I'm bad at ages, and I'd been braced for a schoolgirl in a leather miniskirt, but this woman had to be twenty-eight or twenty-nine, surely. I said quietly, "You're Emilia. He never told me your last name."

When she turned to face me, I saw that her nose must have been broken once, and not set quite right. The effect was oddly attractive, the bumpy bridge lending strength and age to a face whose adult bone structure had not yet finished its work. Only her eyes were a full-grown woman's eyes, an old woman's eyes just now. An intelligent, ordinary face that grief had turned shockingly beautiful.

"It's Rossi," she said. "Emily Rossi." Her voice was low, with the muffled evenness that comes with fighting not to cry. "Please, is there any chance at all that you could be Jacob Holtz?"

"Sam called me Jake," I answered. "We can go now."

As we started to move away, she paused and looked back at the rabbi, who was still telling Mike and Sarah what they felt about their loss. We could smell the raw earth from where we stood. She said softly, "I imagined going up to them, talking with them, letting them know that I loved him, too, that he didn't die alone. But he did, he did, and I'd never have the courage anyway." The back of her neck seemed as vulnerable as a small child's. She said, "He always called me Emilia."

Being an executor means, finally, cleaning the place up. In a legal sense, there wasn't that much for me to do, once the police had finally unsealed the apartment and released Sam's body for burial. Bills paid off, bank account closed out, credit cards canceled, Mike and Sarah's names replacing his on God knows how many computers—how little it takes, after all, to delete us from the Great Database. A heavenly keystroke, no more.

But somebody has to clean up, and the landlord was anxious to have Sam's apartment empty, ready to be rented again for quadruple what Sam had been paying. I spent all day every day for more than three weeks at the apartment, sorting my friend's possessions into ever-more meaningless heaps, then starting over with a new system for determining what went or stayed. With electricity and telephone long since cut off, the place remained cold even when the sun was shining in the windows, and tumultuous Columbus Avenue outside looked so remote, so unattainable, that I felt like an astronaut marooned on the moon.

Emily Rossi—Sam's Emilia—came all the way from New Jersey almost every day, inventing assignments for herself as a partial cover. She usually arrived at the apartment around noon; though sometimes she would bring a sleeping bag and a cassette player—and Millamant, whom Marianne was happy to relinquish—stay the night, and be at work before I got there. I was uneasy about that, but Emilia liked it. "I was always happy here," she said. "This was my safe place, with Sam. I want to be here as long as I can."

I was grateful for her presence, in part because she was far less sentimental than I about most of Sam's belongings. Not all of them: once she had been folding and setting aside clothes for donation (gangster suit apart, his wardrobe could have been worn by the average British prime minister), when I returned from one more trek through the uncharted depths of The Dark Continent to find her rocking back and forth, dry-eyed, holding a gray silk shirt tightly against her cheek.

"The first time he ever held me," she whispered. "Look," and she turned the shirt so that I could see the scattering of faded brown stains on one sleeve. "My blood," Emilia said. "It got all over him, but he never even noticed."

I stared at her. She said, "There was a man. I stopped seeing him before I ever met Sam. He followed me. He caught me on the street one day—downtown, near Port Authority." She touched her nose quickly, and then the area around her left eye. "I don't know how I got away from him. I knew somebody at *Ceilidh*, but I don't remember going there. The only thing I'm clear on, even today, is that somebody was holding me, washing my face, talking to me, so gently. It turned out to be Sam."

She kept turning the shirt in her hands, revealing other bloodstains. "He called the police, he called an ambulance, he went with me to the hospital. And when they wouldn't keep me, even overnight, he took me home with him and fed me, and gave me his bed. I stayed three days."

"It's the feeding part that awes me," I said. "I could see everything else, but Sam didn't cook for anybody. Sam didn't even make coffee."

"Chinese takeout. Mexican takeout. For a special treat, sushi." She smiled then, sniffling only slightly. "He took care of me, Jake. I wasn't used to it, it made me really nervous for a while." She turned sharply away from me, looking toward the corner where the bed had stood. "I was getting used to it, though. Tell me some more about how he was in high school."

So I told her more, day by day, as we worked, and the apartment grew emptier and even colder, and somehow smaller. I told her about writing songs, doing homework together, playing silly board games late at night and about trying to sneak into jazz clubs too young to be admitted legally. I told her everything I could about what it was like to see him dance at seventeen. In return, Emilia told me about Adventures.

"The phone would ring late at night, and I'd hear this hissing, sinister, Bulgarian secret-service voice telling me to be at Penn Station or Grand Central with a rose in my teeth at nine the next morning, and to look for a man in dark glasses carrying an umbrella, a rubber duck, and a rolled-up copy of *Der Spiegel*. And we'd skulk around the station, with people staring at us, until we met, and wind up taking Amtrak to anywhere—to Tarrytown or Rhinecliff or Annandale—still being spies on the Orient Express the whole way. We'd spend the night, go out on a river tour, visit the old estates and museums, buy really dumb souvenirs, and never once break character until we walked out of the station again—back in the city, back in real life. And that was an Adventure."

Her eyes never filled when she talked to me about their outings, but they stopped seeing me, stopped seeing Millamant roaming her old home step by crouching step, stalking ghosts. Emilia's eyes were doing just the same. "We took turns—one time I rented a car and took him to the caverns in Schoharie

County, up near Cobleskill. We were agents who didn't speak each other's language, so we had to make up other ways to communicate." Millamant climbed into her lap, batted at her chin, bit it lightly, and put her paws on Emilia's shoulders. Emilia put her aside, but she kept coming back, meowing fiercely.

It lasted almost a year and a half, counting two separate weeks of vacation: one spent being international spies in Saratoga Springs, and one being contract assassins trailing a famously vicious theater critic who lived in Kingston. "We were always aliens, one way or another, always foreigners, outsiders, Martians. That was the whole thing about Adventures—just having each other, and our secret mission."

On the last day, with everything of Sam's packed up, sold, given away, donated or dumped, and the apartment echoing, even with our breath, we made one last pass through the shrunken Dark Continent in search of Sam's guitar. We never found it. I still worry over that, at very odd hours, wondering whether he might have given it up because of what I said to him on that bad night long ago. I swept the floor while Emilia picked up our own debris and shoe-horned an unusually recalcitrant Millamant into her traveling case. Then we hugged each other good-bye, and stood back, awkward and unhappy, in that cold, empty place.

"Write," she said. "Please." I nodded, and Emily said, "There's only you for me to talk to about him now."

I hugged her again. Inside the case Millamant was making a sound like a jammed garbage disposal, and Emilia laughed, bending to admonish her through the wire mesh. Her dark hair was gray with dust, but she looked very young in that moment, even her eyes.

For the next year—almost two—we wrote more letters than I've ever exchanged with anyone except Sam, and that includes anybody I ever married. How Emilia managed to balance her output against her newspaper work, I can't guess; it was tricky enough for me—especially once *Christmas Carol* rehearsals started—to drag myself out of Bob Cratchit's intolerably benign consciousness back into my own sullen grief. And after wretched Cratchit came Canon Chasuble, Mr. Peachum, Grandpa Vanderhof, *St. Joan*'s Earl of Warwick . . . actually that wasn't a bad run of roles, thinking about it. Though I should have at least read for Macheath.

But I still wrote to Emilia two and three times a week, unearthing for her sake, and my own, moments as long forgotten as Sam's youthful terror of FBI agents coming back to interrogate his father once more about Mike's ten-minute membership in the Communist Party. I rooted through tattered, filthy cardboard boxes to find fragments of the songs we'd written together. I even woke her up one night, calling with a remembrance of our one attempt at fishing, out on Sheepshead Bay, that couldn't wait until morning. Irrational, surely, but I was suddenly afraid of forgetting for another forty years.

Emilia wrote to me about living without Adventures. She wrote about answering the phone at work or at home, knowing that she might hear any voice on the planet except the whisper of the mad Bulgarian spy, enticing her away to ridiculous escapades in the dark wilds of the Catskills.

> But I don't believe it, any of it, either way. I don't believe that it'll be him on the phone, but at the same time I still can't believe that I won't ever hear him again. Nothing makes sense. I do my work, and I go home, and I cook my meals and eat them, and I pick up the phone when it rings, but I'm really always waiting for the call after this one. . . .

Once she wrote, "Thank you for always calling me Emilia. I liked her so much—she was so passionate and adventurous, so different from Emily. I was sure Emilia died with Sam, but now I don't know. Maybe not."

For my part, writing usually at night, often when rehearsals had run late and I was weary enough that memory and language both tangled with dream, the stories I told of Sam and myself were as true as phoenixes, as imaginary as computers. Things we had done flowed together with things we had always meant to do, things that I think I felt we *would* have done, once Emilia believed them. I recalled for her the time that Sam had withered a school bully with a retort so eviscerating that it would have gotten us both killed had it ever actually been spoken. I even dredged up a certain Adventure of our own, in which we tracked a celebrated Russian poet (recognized crossing Ninth Avenue by Sam, of course) back to his hotel, and then—at Sam's insistence—returned early the next morning to haunt the elevator until he came down to breakfast, which we wound up sharing with him. "He defected a few days later, and got a university gig in San Diego. Sam always felt it was the Froot Loops that did it." Well, Sam did spot the poet on the street, and we did follow him until we lost him in Macy's. And Russian poets did defect, and maybe it all practically happened just that way. Why shouldn't it have?

What Emilia was after in my memories of Sam, what she needed to live on, was no different from what I needed still: not facts, but the accuracy under and around and beyond facts. Not a recital of events—not even honesty—but truth. Resumés have their place, but there's no nourishment in them.

Emilia arrived weary at the Oakland Airport, looking as small and windblown as she had at Sam's funeral. But her eyes were bright, and when she smiled to recognize me I saw her meeting my friend, her lover, in Penn Station to embark on one more Adventure. It wasn't entirely meant for me, that smile.

Millamant herself had apparently been quite docile on the flight from New York—even banging around on the luggage conveyor belt didn't seem to have fazed her. Uncaged in my house, she didn't exhibit any of the usual edginess of a cat in strange surroundings: she stretched here, strolled there, leisurely investigated this and that, as though getting reacquainted, and finally curled herself in the one good chair, plainly waiting for the floor show to begin. I looked at Emilia, who shrugged and said, "Like the washing machine when the repairman arrives. Wait. You'll see."

"See what? What the Baptist hell are we waiting for?"

"Dinner," Emilia said firmly. "Take me out to that Caribbean place—I don't know the name. The one where you took Sam."

I hadn't been back since the time we celebrated his being down to two cigarettes a day. I ordered the *rópa vieja* again. I don't remember what Emilia had. We talked about Sam, and about her work for the Bergen County newspaper—she'd recently won a state journalism award for a series on day-care facilities—and I went into serious detail regarding the technical and social inadequacies of the Pacific Rep's new artistic director. We didn't discuss Millamant at all.

The evening was warm, and there was one of those glossy, perfect half-moons that seem too brilliant for their size. We walked home the long way, so that I could show Emilia the little park where Sam had told me about her. We sat on the swings, as I'd done with Sam, and she told me then, "He lied about his age, you know. I didn't realize it until you told me you were two months younger. He'd been taking seven years off, all the time I knew him. As though it would have mattered to me."

I'd had a second margarita with dinner. I said, "He was two months and eleven days older than I am. We were both born just after three in the morning, did he ever tell you that? I was about an ounce and a half heavier." And *whoosh*, I was crying. I didn't *start* to cry—I *was* crying, and I was always going to be crying. Emilia held me without a word, as I'd once held Sam when he wept just as hopelessly, just as endlessly. I have no idea how long it went on. When it stopped, we walked the rest of the way in silence, but Emilia tucked her arm through mine.

Back home, we settled in the kitchen (which is bigger and more comfortable than my living room) with a couple of cappuccinos. The director ex-wife took the piano, but I hung on to the espresso machine. Emilia said, "I was thinking on the flight—you and I have already known each other longer than I knew Sam. We had such a short time."

"You learned things about him I never bothered to find out in forty years. I thought we had forever."

Emilia was silent for a while, sipping her coffee. Then she said, very softly, not looking at me, "You see, I never thought that. Some way, I always understood that there wasn't going to be a happy ending for us. I never said it to myself, but I *knew*." She did look straight at me then, her eyes clear and unmisted, but her mouth too straight, too determinedly under control. "I think he did, too."

I couldn't think of an answer to that. We chatted a little while longer, and then Emilia went to bed. I stayed up late, reading *Heartbreak House* one more time—no one's ever likely to ask me to play Captain Shotover, but the readiness is all—had one last futile look-around for Millamant, and turned in myself. I slept deeply and contentedly for what seemed like a good fifteen minutes before Emilia shook me out of one of the rare dreams where I know my lines, whispering frantically, "Jake—Jake—come and see, hurry, you have to see! Jake, hurry, it's her!"

The half-moon was shining so brightly on the kitchen table that I could see the little sticky rings where our coffee cups had been. I remember that, just as I remember the shuddery hum of the refrigerator and the *bloop* of the leaky faucet, and a faint scratching sound that I couldn't place right away. Just as I remember Millamant dancing.

It's a large table, older than I am, and it lurches if you lean on it, let alone dance. I don't know how Millamant even climbed up, arthritic back leg and all, but there she floated, there she spun, tumbling this way, sailing that, one minute a kitten, the next a kite; moving so lightly, and with such precision, that the table never rocked once, but seemed to be the one moving impossibly fast, while Millamant drifted over it as slowly as she chose, hanging in the air for exactly as long as she chose. She was so old that her back claws no longer retracted entirely—that was the scratching noise—but she danced the way human beings have always dreamed of dancing, and never have, not the best of them. No one has ever danced like Millamant.

Neither of us could look away, but Emilia leaned close and whispered, "I've seen her three times. I couldn't talk about it on the phone." Her face was absolutely without color.

Millamant stopped so suddenly that both Emilia and I leaned toward her, as though it had been the planet that halted. Millamant dropped down onto all fours, paced to the edge of the table and stood looking at us out of once-golden eyes gone almost tea-brown with age. She was breathing rapidly, and trembling all over. She said, "Emilia. Jake."

How can I say what it was like? To hear a cat speak—to hear a cat speak our names—to hear a cat speak them in a voice that was unmistakably Sam's voice, and yet not Sam's, not a voice at all. Her mouth remained slightly open, but her jaws did not move: the words were coming through her, not out of her, without inflection, without any sort of cadence, without any trace of a homemade English accent. Millamant said, "Jake. Clean your glasses."

I wear glasses, except onstage, and the lenses are always messier than I ever notice. It used to drive Sam crazy. I took them off. Millamant—or what was using Millamant—said, "I love you, Emilia."

Beside me, Emilia's breath simply stopped. I didn't dare look at her. I had all I could do to babble idiotically, "Sam? Sam? Where have you *been*? Sam, are you really *in* there?"

At that Millamant actually seemed to raise an eyebrow, which was unlikely, since cats don't have eyebrows. She—Sam—*it* said quite clearly, "You want I should wave?" And she did raise a front paw to gesture in my direction. Her ears were flicking and crumpling strangely, as though someone who didn't know how a cat's ears work were trying to lay them back. "As to where I've been"—the toneless march of syllables faltered a little—"it comes and goes. Talk to me."

Emilia's face was still so pale that the color on her cheekbones stood out like tribal scars. I don't know what I looked like, but I couldn't make a sound. Emilia took a step forward, her hands out, but Millamant immediately backed away. "Talk to me. Please, talk to me. Tell me why we're all here, tell me anything. Please."

So we sat in the kitchen, Emilia and I, talking to an

old cat as we would have talked to our dear lost friend, solemnly telling her our commonplace news of work and family, of small travels and travails, of his parents in Miami, of how it had been for us in the last two years. Our voices stumbled over each other, often crumbling into tears of still-untrusted joy, then immediately skidding off into broken giggles to hear ourselves earnestly assuring Millamant, "It's been a miserable couple of theater seasons—absolutely nothing you'd have liked." Millamant looked from one to the other of us, her eyes fiercely attentive, sometimes nodding like a marionette. Emilia clutched my hand painfully tightly, but she was smiling. I have never seen a smile like that one of Emilia's ever again.

She was saying, "And Jake and I have been writing and writing to each other, talking on the phone, telling each other everything we remember—things we didn't know we remembered. Things *you* maybe wouldn't remember. Sam, we missed you so. I missed you." When she reached out again, Millamant avoided her touch for a moment; then suddenly yielded and let herself rest between Emilia's hands. The arid, rasping voice said, "Behind the ears. Finally, a body I can dance in, but I can't figure out about scratching."

Nobody said anything for a while. Emilia was totally involved in caressing Millamant, and I was feeling more and more like the most flagrant *voyeur*. I didn't have to look at Emilia's face, or listen to Millamant's purring; merely to watch those yearning hands at work in the thin, patchy fur was to spy on an altogether private matter. I make jokes when I'm edgy. I said to Emilia, "Be careful—he could be a *dybbuk*. It'd be just like him."

Emilia, not knowing the Yiddish word, looked puzzled; but Millamant let out a brief, contemptuous yowl, a feline equivalent of Sam's old *Oh, good night!* snort of disdain. "Of course, I'm not a bloody *dybbuk*! Don't you read Singer? A *dybbuk*'s a wandering soul, demons chasing it all around the universe—it needs a body, a place to hide. Not me—nobody's chasing me." The voice hesitated slightly for a second time. "Except maybe you two."

I looked at Emilia, expecting her to say something. When she didn't, I finally mumbled—just as lamely as it reads—"We needed to talk about you. We didn't have anyone else to talk to."

"If not for Jake," Emilia said. "Sam, if it weren't for Jake, if he hadn't known me at your funeral"—she caught her breath only momentarily on the word—"Sam, I would have disappeared. I'd have gone right on, like always, like everybody else, but I would have disappeared."

Millamant hardly seemed to be listening. She said thoughtfully, "I'll be damned. I'm hungry."

"I'll make you a *quesadilla*," I said, eager to be doing something practical. "Cheese and scallions and Ortega diced chilies—I've still got a can from the last time you were here. Take me ten minutes."

The look both Millamant and Emilia gave me was pure cat. I said, "Oh. Right. Wet or dry?"

Nothing in life—nothing even in Shakespeare—adequately prepares you for the experience of opening a can of Whiskas with Bits O' Beef for your closest friend, who's been dead for two years. Millamant ambled over to the battered stoneware dish that Emilia had brought with her from New York, sniffed once, then dug in with a voracity I'd never seen in either Sam or her. She went through that red-brown glop like a snowplow, and looked around for more.

Scraping the rest into her dish, I couldn't help asking, "How can you be hungry, anyway? Are you the one actually tasting this stuff, or is it all Millamant?"

"Interesting point." The Abyssinian had Whiskas on her nose. "It's Millamant who needs to eat—it's Millamant getting the nourishment—but I think I'm beginning to see why she likes it. Very odd. Sort of the phantom of a memory of taste. A touch of nutmeg would help."

She dived back into her dinner, obliviously, leaving Emilia and me staring at each other in confusion so identical that there was no need to speak, possibly ever again. Emilia finally managed to ask, "What do we do now?" and I answered, "Like a divorce. We work out who gets custody, and who gets visiting rights."

Emilia said, "She doesn't belong to us. She was Sam's cat, and he's . . . returned."

"To take possession, as you might say. Right. We can't even be certain that she's exactly a cat anymore, what with Sam in residence." I realized that I was just this side of hysterical, and closing fast. "Emilia, you'd better take him—her—them—home with you. I'm an actor, I pretend for a living, and this is altogether too much reality for me. You take Millamant home—what I'll do, I'll just call on the weekends, the way we used to do. Sam and I."

I don't know what Emilia would have said—her eyes were definitely voting for scooping up Millamant that very moment and heading for the airport—but the cat herself looked up from an empty dish at that moment to remark, in the mechanical tone I was already coming to accept as Sam, "Calm down, Jake. You're overplaying again."

It happens to be one of my strengths as an actor that I *never* overplay. The man saw me act exactly three times after high school, and that makes him an expert on my style. I was still spluttering as Millamant sat down in the kitchen doorway, curling her tail around her hind legs.

"Well," the voice said. "I'm back. Where I'm back *from*"—and it faltered momentarily, while Millamant's old eyes seemed to lose all definition between iris and pupil—"where I'm back from doesn't go into words. I don't know what it really is, or where—or when. I don't know whether I'm a ghost, or a zombie, or just some kind of seriously perturbed spirit. If I were a *dybbuk*, at least I'd know I was a *dybbuk*, that would be something." Millamant licked the bit of Whiskas off her nose. "But here I am anyway, ready or not. I can talk, I can dance—my God, I can *dance*—and I'm reunited with the only two people in the world who could have summoned me. Or whatever it was you did."

Abruptly she began washing her face, making such a deliberate job of it that I was about to say something pointed about extended dramatic pauses, when Sam spoke again. "But for how long? I could be gone any minute, or I could last as long as Millamant lasts—and *she* could go any minute herself. What happens then? Do I go off to kitty heaven with her—

or do I find myself in Jake's blender? One of Emilia's angelfish? What happens then?"

Nobody answered. Millamant sat up higher on her haunches, until she looked like the classic Egyptian statue of Bastet, the cat goddess. Out of her mouth Sam said very quietly, "We don't know. We have no idea. I certainly wish somebody had read the instruction manual."

"There wasn't any manual," I said. "We didn't know we were summoning you—we didn't know we were doing anything except missing you, and trying to comfort ourselves the best we could." I was calming down, and paradoxically irritable with it. "Not everybody has people wishing for him so hard that they snatch him right back from death. I'm sorry if we woke you."

"Oh, I was awake." The cold voice was still soft and faraway. "Or maybe not truly awake, but you can't quite get to sleep, either. Jake . . . Emilia . . . I can't tell you what it's like. I'm not even sure whether it's death—or maybe that's it, that's just it, that's really the way death is. I can't tell you."

"Don't," Emilia whispered. She picked Millamant up again and held her close against her breast, not petting her.

Sam said, "It's like the snow on a TV set, when the cable's out. People just sit watching the screen, expecting the picture to come back—they'll sit there for an hour, more, waiting for all those whirling, crackling white particles to shape themselves back into a face, a car, a box of cereal—*something*. Try to think how it might feel to be one of those particles." He said nothing more for a moment, and then added, "It's not like that but try to imagine it anyway."

Whereupon Millamant fell asleep in Emilia's arms, and was carried off to bed in the guest room. She sauntered out the next morning, looking demurely pleased with herself, shared Emilia's yogurt, topped that off with an entire can of Chunky Chicken, went back to sleep on a fragrant pile of new-dried laundry, woke presently, and came to find me in the living room, settle briskly onto my lap and issue instructions. Fondling your best friend's tummy and scratching his vibrating throat for a solid hour at a time may possibly be weirder than responding to his demand for more kibble. I'm still not sure.

Presently he remarked, in that voice that wasn't him and wasn't human, and was yet somehow Sam, "In case I haven't said it, I'm very happy to see you, Jake."

"I'm happy to see you, too." I stopped petting him once we were talking: it felt wrong. "I just wish I could . . . *see* you."

Sam didn't laugh—I don't think he could—but a sort of odd grumbly ripple ran through Millamant's body. "You surprise me. You didn't actually plan to have me come back with fleas and hair balls?"

"Just like old times," I said, and Millamant did the ripple thing again. "Truth is, I think it's easier to accept you like this than it would be if you'd showed up in some other person's body. You always had a lot in common with Millamant."

"Did, didn't I?" For a moment the words were almost lost in Millamant's deep purr. "We both love peach yogurt, and having things on our own terms. But I couldn't dance like Millamant the best day I ever saw. Jake, you don't *know*—when she was a kitten, pouncing and skittering around the apartment, I used to watch her for hours, wondering if it wasn't too late, if I could still make my body learn something from her that it never could learn from anyone else. Even now, old as she is, you can't imagine how it feels. . . ." He was silent for so long that I thought Millamant must have fallen asleep once more; but then he said suddenly, "Jake. Maybe you should send me back."

Emilia was in the guest bedroom, talking on the phone to her editor in New Jersey, so there was just me to be flabbergasted. When I had words again, I said, "Send you? We don't even know how you got here in the first place, and you don't know where *back* is. We couldn't send you anywhere the BMT doesn't run." No furry ripple out of Millamant. "Why would you want to? To leave us again?"

"I don't ever want to leave." Millamant's dull claws dug harder into my leg than they should have been able to. "If I were in a rat's body, a cockroach's body, I'd want to stay here with you, with Emilia.

But it feels strange here. Not wrong, but not—not *proper*. I don't mean me inhabiting a cat—I mean me still being me, Sam Kagan still aware that I'm Sam Kagan. However you look at it, this is a damn afterlife, Jake, and I don't believe in an afterlife. Dead or alive, I don't."

"And being part of the snow on a television screen, that's an improvement? That's proper?"

Sam didn't answer for a time. Millamant purred drowsily between my hands, and my Betty Boop clock ticked (at certain times of day, you can almost pretend she's dancing the Charleston), and in the guest bedroom Emilia laughed at something. Finally Sam said, "You see, I don't think I was always going to be TV snow. There was more to it. I can't tell you how I knew that. I just did."

I unhooked a rear claw from my thigh. "Purgatory as a function of the cable system. Makes sense, in a really dumb way."

Sam said, "There was more. I don't know that I missed anything much, but there was more coming. And if it's an afterlife, then the word means something they never told us about. I don't think there *is* a word for it—what I was waiting for. But it wasn't this."

Emilia hung up and came out to us then, and Millamant stopped talking. Instead, she leaped down from my lap, landing with the precise abandon of a cat ten years younger, and began to dance. Last night it had been for herself—at least, until we showed up—this time the dance was entirely for us, Sam showing off joyously, taking the whole room as his stage, as Millamant swam in the air from chair to bookcase and flashed like a dragonfly between bookcase and stereo, setting a rack of tape cassettes vibrating like castanets. Partnering my furniture, she swung around my three-foot-high Yoruba fetish, mimicking Gene Kelly in *Singin' in the Rain*; then whirled across the room by spinning bounds, only to slow to a liquidly sensuous cat-waltz in and out of the striped shadows of my window blinds. I couldn't remember ever seeing Sam dance like that: so much in authority that he could afford to release his body on its own recognizance. Millamant finished with a sudden astonishing flare of pirouettes from a standing start, and *jetéed* her way into Emilia's lap, where she purred and panted and said nothing. Emilia petted her and looked at me, and we didn't say anything either.

Neither of us said anything after that about Emilia's taking Sam home with her. She spent all ten days of her leave like an inheritance at my house. Sly smiles, grotesquely rolled eyes and hasty thumbs-up signs from my neighbors made their opinion of my new little fling eminently clear. I really can't blame them: we almost never went out, except for a meal or a brief walk, and we must have seemed completely absorbed in one another when they saw us at all. But what they'd have thought of the hours we passed, day and night, watching an old Abyssinian cat dance all over my house, let alone arguing with the cat about afterlives and the last World Series . . . no, it would have broken their hearts if I'd told them. Mine is a very dull neighborhood.

There was never a chance of anything happening between us, Emilia and me. We had grown far too close to be lovers: we were almost brother and sister in Sam, if that makes any sense at all. Once, midway through her visit, she was ironing her clothes in the kitchen when I came in to fill the cat dish and the water bowl. She watched in silence until I was done, and then she said with a sudden half-strangled violence, "I hate this! I can't bear to see you doing that, putting food down for him. It's not"—and she seemed to be fighting her own throat for a word—"it's not *honest*!"

We stared at each other across the ironing board. I said slowly, "Honest? How did honesty get into this?"

"Did I say that?" She scrubbed absently at her forehead with the back of her hand. "I don't know, I don't know what I meant. If he's Sam, then he shouldn't be eating on the floor, and if he's Millamant, then he shouldn't be making her dance all the time. She's old, Jake, and she's got arthritis, and Sam's dancing her like a child making his toys fly and fight. And it's so beautiful, and he's so *happy*—and I never saw him dance, the way you did, and I can't believe how beautiful . . ."

She didn't start to cry. Emilia doesn't cry. What happens is that she loses speech—when Sam died, she couldn't speak for three days—and the few sounds she does make are not your business or mine. I went to her then, and she buried her face in the ruinous gray cardigan I wear around the house, and we just stood together without speaking. And yes, all right, there was an instant when she held me hard, tilting her head back so we could look at each other. I felt very cold, and my lips started to tingle most painfully. But neither of us moved. We stood there, very deliberately letting the moment pass, feeling it pass, more united in that wordless choice than we could have been in any other way. Emilia went back to folding her ironing, and I took the garbage out and paid some bills.

Then I spent some time studying Millamant. The cat didn't seem to be suffering, nor to object to being sported and soared and exalted all around my house, day and night. But the bad back leg was plainly lamer than ever; her eyes were streaked and her claws ragged and broken, and for all the serious eating she was doing, she was thinner than she had arrived, if you looked. Playing host to Sam—playing barre and floor, costume, makeup, mirror to Sam, more accurately—was literally consuming her. I couldn't know whether she understood that or not. It didn't matter to me. That was the terrible thing, and all I can say is that at least I knew it was terrible.

The next evening was a warm one, pleasantly poignant with the smell of my next-door neighbor's jasmine, and of distant rain. Sam/Millamant hadn't danced at all that day, but had spent it necking and nuzzling with Emilia, taking naps with her and exchanging murmured *do-you-remembers*. We sat together on my front steps: a perfectly ordinary couple with a drowsy old cat in the long California twilight. I made small talk, fixed small snacks, felt my throat getting smaller and smaller, and finally blurted, "You were right. I can't say if it's honest or not, but it's no good. What do we do about it?"

Emilia petted Millamant and didn't meet my eyes. Three high school boys ambled past, slamming a basketball into one another's chests by turns, their talk as incomprehensible as Czech or Tamil, and strangely more foreign. I said again, "Sam, it's no good. I don't mean for Millamant—I mean for you, for your *ka* or your karma, or whatever I'm talking to right now. This can't be what you're supposed to be . . . doing, I guess. Emilia made me see."

In a very small voice, still not looking at me, Emilia said, "I changed my mind." I remember to this day how sad she sounded, and how neither Sam nor I paid any attention to her. An errant Irish setter, outrunning his jogger mistress, wandered up to say hello to everybody's crotch, but Millamant spat viciously and scratched his nose as Sam said, "I told you you ought to send me back. I did tell you, Jake."

I started to answer him, but Emilia interrupted. "No," she said, much louder now. "No, I don't care, I *can't*, never mind what I said. I don't care about Millamant, I don't care about anybody except Sam. I just want Sam back, any way I can have him. *Any* way. It's disgraceful, I know it's disgraceful, and I don't care."

She bent over Millamant, who slipped away from

her as a yellow-haired young man in a Grateful Dead T-shirt and Bermuda shorts strode by, pumping his arms like a power-walker, totally absorbed in laughing, comradely conversation with his Walkman. I still see him, most days—it's been years now. Sometimes he's quite angry with the Walkman, but mostly he laughs.

Very gently for a voice out of a P.A. system in bad repair, Sam said, "He's right, Emilia. And you were right the first time. I have to go."

"Go where?" she cried. "You don't even know, you said so yourself. You could end up someplace worse than your damn TV screen—you could lose yourself for good, no Sam anymore, in the whole universe, not the least bit of Sam, not ever, not ever." She stopped herself with a jolt that was actually audible—you could hear it in her chest. Newspaper reporters probably aren't allowed hysterics. With actors it's part of the Equity contract.

"Maybe that's the idea." Millamant sat down and scratched—very professionally, I noticed. "Maybe that's it—maybe you're not supposed to come back as the least bit of yourself, but to be completely scattered, diffused, starting over as someone utterly different. I almost like that." And the mechanical voice sounded in that moment more like *my* Sam—thoughtful, amused, truly savoring doubt—than it ever had.

Emilia was hugging herself, rocking herself slightly. She said, "I couldn't bear to lose you twice. I'm telling you now, I have no shame, I don't care. I don't care if you show up as a—an electric can opener. Don't leave me again, Sam."

Only a few of the cars going by had turned their headlights on, but all the porch lights were lit now, and the lawn sprinklers hissing to life, and I could smell Vietnamese cooking two houses down, and Indian cooking clear across the street. Two young women in identical jogging suits walked past, each carrying a pizza box and a six-pack. Millamant walked slowly to Emilia, climbed into her lap and stood up—surprisingly firm on the bad back leg—to put her paws on each side of Emilia's neck.

"Matter can neither be created nor destroyed,"

Sam said. "Didn't they teach you that in high school, out in frontier Metuchen? *Listen*!" for she had turned her head away and would not even touch Millamant. "*Listen*—when I was a speck, a dot, nothing but a flicker of TV snow, I knew you. Do you understand me? By the time you and Jake got me back here, I had already forgotten my own name, I'd forgotten that there was ever such an idea as Sam Kagan. But I was a speck that remembered Emilia Rossi's birthday, remembered that Emilia Rossi loves cantaloupe and roast potatoes and bittersweet chocolate, and absolutely cannot abide football, her cousin Teddy, or Wagner. There's no way in this universe that I could be reduced to something so microscopic, so anonymous that it wouldn't know Emilia Rossi. If they give my atoms a fast shuffle and shake most of them out on some other planet, there'll still be one or two atoms madly determined to evolve into something that can carve *Emilia Rossi* on a tree. Or whatever they've got on the damn planet. I promise you, that's the truth. Are you listening to me, Emilia?"

"I'm listening," she said dully. She still would not look at Millamant. "You'll never forget me, wherever you are—or *whatever*. Wonderful. But you're leaving."

Millamant bumped her head hard against Emilia's chin, forcing her to turn her head. Sam said, "I don't belong here. You knew it before Jake did—probably before I knew myself. It's all I want in any world, but it's not right. Let me go, Emilia."

"Let you go?" Emilia was so outraged that she stood up, dumping Millamant off her lap. "What hold did I ever have on you, living or dead? What about Jake? Why don't you ask Jake if he'd be so kind as to . . ." And her voice went. Completely. I told you it happens with Emilia.

I put my arms around her. An old couple passing by nodded benignly at us through the dusk. I looked at my friend in the ancient eyes of a cat, and I said, "She's not going to understand. If you're going, go."

"You'll explain to her?" The robot voice couldn't possibly sound desperate, any more than it could convey anger or love, but I felt Sam's grief in my body, even so. "You'll make her see?"

"I won't make her do anything." I ached for Sam, but I was holding Emilia. "I'll do the best I can. Go already."

Millamant didn't approach Emilia again, so she never saw the last look that Sam gave her. But I did, and I told her about it afterward. Then Millamant scampered up the steps, lightly as a kitten, and began to dance.

My front porch could be better described as a catwalk with a railing. You can't even rock on it in comfort—your feet keep hitting things—and it's the last place you'd imagine as a dance floor, even for a small domestic animal. But Sam used to tell me, when we were young and I'd been awed by the flamboyance of some performer's style, "Good *night,* Jake, anybody can throw himself around Lincoln Center—all that takes is space and a little energy. The real ones can dance in a broom closet; they can stand on line at a checkout counter and be dancing right there. The real ones." And Millamant was a real dancer, that one last time on my checkout line of a porch.

I can't be sure of what I saw through the gathering

dark then and the gathering years now. Millamant seemed to me to be moving almost on point, if you can imagine that in a cat, but moving with a kind of ardent restraint in which every stillness implied a leap at the throat, and violence trembled in the shadow of rigor. At moments she appeared to be standing completely motionless, letting the twilight dance around her, courting her like a proper partner. There should have been a moon, but there wasn't: only my rust-colored bug light to catch the glitter of her eyes and the ripple of her fur. So the one thing I *am* certain about, even at this dim distance, is that that dance was entirely for Emilia. Not for me, not for Emilia and me together, like that first time. Emilia.

She wouldn't look at first. She turned her head completely away, staring blindly back at the street, one hand clenching white on a fold of my sweater. So something else I can't say is just when the dance took hold of her, drawing her gently home to what Sam—and Millamant, Millamant, too—were telling her forever. All I know is that she was crouched beside me, paying such attention, *paying,* as I never paid to my wives, my directors, or to Sam himself, at the moment when someone's headlights played briefly over us and it was only Millamant there, limping down the steps to clamber heavily into Emilia's lap and lie there, not purring. Only old Abyssinian Millamant, tired and lame, and uninhabited.

I also don't remember when it was that I said, "He made us let him go. He danced us away from thinking about him, holding him. Just for that little, but it was all he needed." Emilia didn't answer. The lighted kitchens along my street were long dark when I finally got her into the house and put her to bed.

That was long ago. Emilia went back to New Jersey with Millamant and married a nice special-education teacher named Philip, some years later. She didn't write to me for some time after her return, but she telephoned when Millamant died. Gradually we took up our correspondence again, though Sam was as notably absent from it as he had once been its prime mover. I sent a gift when the boy was born: a complete Shakespeare and a *Baseball Encyclopedia.* If those don't cover a growing child's major emotional needs, he's on his own.

Me, I haven't yet been summoned to play Captain Shotover—or Lear, either—but the Falstaffs have started coming lately, and the James Tyrones, and I did do a bloody good Uncle Vanya in Ashland one summer. And I got to New York for the first time in decades, for a get-killed-early role in a big-budget thing where they blew up the Holland Tunnel at the climax. I rather liked that one.

I stayed with Emilia and Philip over a weekend after my part of the shooting was over. They live in an old two-family house in a working-class neighborhood of Secaucus. Secaucus still has one of those, a working class. The place could use a new roof, and there's a draft in the kitchen that Philip hasn't been able to trace down yet. It's a good house, with a black kitten named Rita, for Rita Hayworth. Philip loves old movies and early music.

On the day I left, Emilia and I sat in the kitchen while she gave Alex his lunch. Alex was ten-and-a-half months old then, with a rapturous smile and the table manners of a Hell's Angel. But today he was in one of his dreamy, contemplative moods, and made no difficulties over the brown stuff, which he normally despised, or the green stuff, which he preferred to play with. I sat in a patch of sunlight, watching the two of them. Emilia's gained a little weight, but on her it looks good, and there's a warmth under her pale skin. Marriage suits her. Secaucus suits her.

I think I was actually half asleep when she turned suddenly to me and said, "You think I don't think about him."

"Actually, I hope you don't," I said, rather feebly. "I try not to, myself."

"There isn't a day," Emilia said. "Not one." She wiped Alex's mouth and took advantage of his meditations to slip some of the yellow stuff into him. "Philip always knows, but he doesn't mind. He's a good man."

"Does he know the whole story? What can happen when you think too much about someone?"

She shook her head without answering. When

Alex had reached capacity and was looking remarkably like Sidney Greenstreet in the noonday sun of Casablanca, she took him to his crib, singing "This Time the Dream's on Me" softly as she set him down, already asleep. It was one of Sam's favorite old songs, and she knew I knew. I looked down at Alex and said, "Nice legs. You think there might be a dancer at the other end of them?"

Emilia shook her head quickly. "No, absolutely. He's very much Philip's child. He'll probably play football and grow up to be an ACLU lawyer, and a good thing, too. I'm not going to make him into my dreams of Sam." We tiptoed out of the room, and she gave me one of the heavy black beers for which Philip and I—and Sam, too, for that matter—shared a taste. She said clearly and firmly, "Alex is real. Philip is real. Sam is dead. My dreams are my own business. I can live with them."

"And you never wonder—"

She cut me off immediately, her eyes steady on mine, but her mouth going tight. "I don't wonder, Jake. I can't afford it."

She seemed about to say something more, but the doorbell interrupted her. When she answered it, there stood a small brown girl, no older than five or six, on the step, asking eagerly before the door was fully open, "Miz Larsen, can I play with Alex now?" She looked Filipina, and she was dressed, not in the T-shirt and jeans which children are born wearing these days, but in a white blouse and a dark woolen skirt, as though she were going to church or to visit grandparents. But her accent was unadulterated New Jersey, born and bred.

Emilia smiled at her. "He's having his nap, Luz. Come back in an hour or so. Do you know how long an hour is?"

"My brother knows hours," Luz said proudly. "Okay. 'Bye." She turned away, and Emilia closed the door, still smiling.

"Luz lives a block down from us," she said softly. "She's been crazy about Alex from the day he was born, and he adores her. She's over here almost every day, after school, talking to him, carrying him, inventing games to make him laugh. I'm sure the first real word he says will be *Luz*."

She was talking fast, almost chattering, which is not something Emilia does. We looked at each other in a way that we hadn't since I'd been there. Emilia turned away, and then stood quite still, staring through a front window. Without turning, she beckoned, and I joined her.

On the sidewalk in front of the house, little Luz was dancing.

Not ballet, of course; not the self-consciousness that suggested lessons of any sort. Her movements were just this side of the jump-and-whirl of hopscotch, and there were moments when she might have been skipping double-Dutch without the ropes. But it was dancing, pure and private, and there was music to it—you had only to look at the intense brown face for that. Luz was hearing music, and to watch her for even a little time was to hear it too.

"Every day," Emilia said. "Her parents don't know—I asked them. She waits for Alex to wake up, and while she waits she dances. Nowhere else, just here. I hoped you'd see."

Luz never looked up toward the house, toward us.

I said, "She doesn't dance like Millamant." Emilia didn't bother to answer anything that dumb. We watched a while longer before I said, "He told you, whatever became of him—his soul, his spirit, his molecules—he'd always know you. But he didn't say whether you'd know him."

"It doesn't matter," Emilia said. She took my arm, hugging it tightly, and her face was as bright and young as the child's. "Jake, Jake, it doesn't matter whether I know him or not. It doesn't *matter*."

Luz was still dancing on the sidewalk when the taxi came to take me to the train station. I said goodbye as I walked past her, trying not to stare. But she danced me escort to the cab door, and I looked into her eyes as I got in, and as we drove away. And what I think I know, I think I know, and it doesn't matter at all.